Birthday Surprise

"Hi! I'm Sportacus!

Do you want to know what happened when my friends tried to organise my birthday party? They learned a special lesson about working together – it's too bad Robbie Rotten tried to spoil the day!"

As you read the story, why not try the games and activities you find along the way? No one's lazy in LazyTown and you can be just like Sportacus and his friends!

It was soon to be a special day in LazyTown – but Ziggy couldn't remember why!

"Hi Ziggy," said Stingy as they met in the Town Square. "Why do you have a ribbon on your finger?"

"It's to remind me of something that's very important," Ziggy told him.

"Tell me, tell me. What is it?" Stingy asked.

Ziggy blushed. "I kinda forgot."

The friends' mystery was solved when Trixie came along with a ribbon on **her** finger!

"It's to remind me of tomorrow," Trixie said.

"It's Sportacus's birthday!"

"We should tell the others," Ziggy decided. "Maybe they forgot too, huh?"

The friends ran to Pixel's house, where he and Stephanie were playing video games. Clever Stephanie had remembered Sportacus's birthday.

"Why don't we throw him the greatest party ever?" she suggested.

What a great idea!

The kids began to plan the birthday party.

Stingy thought it should be at his house where there was a fountain and a beautiful lawn. But Stephanie thought it would be better at the sports field. "Sportacus would love to play sports on his birthday," she explained.

Before long, the friends were arguing . . . and SOMEBODY was listening in.

It was **Robbie Rotten** of course!

Nobody could agree where Sportacus's party should be held!

Suddenly, Stingy lost his temper. He drew a chalk line on the ground, dividing him and Pixel from Stephanie, Ziggy and Trixie.

"You stay on that side and never come to my house again," he huffed. "If I had my way, I would build a wall so big I would never see you or even smell you again!"

Stingy had given nosy Robbie a ROTTEN idea. He would build a wall that would split the town in half!

"They'll never meet again, they'll never play again. Peace and quiet in LazyTown!"

Robbie plotted as he disguised himself **as a builder.**

9

Stingy and Pixel didn't like to
argue with their friends and they
began to feel bad.

"We shouldn't be fighting," said
Pixel. "We should all be friends.
I think we should apologise."

Stingy agreed. "I'll work on my
apology now and have it ready
in the morning."

Stephanie was feeling the same way.
"I hope that we will be friends tomorrow,"
she sang as she gazed out of her window.

10

Tomorrow was, after all, Sportacus's special day.

But Robbie had other plans...

"I'm so smart, I'm so sneaky and so bad!" he muttered as he worked through the night . . .

*T*he next day, Stingy and Pixel went to apologise to their friends.

Stingy had stayed up late to write the apology and he wanted it to be just right.

hereby offer and deliver my official apology," he read, as –

OOMF!

He and Pixel walked straight into a huge wall!

"What's this?" Stingy stared at the wall – and its rotten builder.

"This is a big wall," said the builder, "can't you see? The others asked for it. Pinky, Swinky, Nixy . . ."

Stephanie, Ziggy and Trixie had asked for the wall to be built? Stingy and Pixel couldn't believe it!

"They said something about never wanting to see you again," the rotten builder added for good measure. But before Stingy or Pixel could reply, the builder had snatched his tools and sneaked away.

13

On the other side of the wall Stephanie was in a much happier mood. She skipped into town making plans for the party.

"We'll need streamers," she wrote in her diary. "Oh, and balloons . . . and –"

OOMF!

Stephanie bumped into the wall and fell down with a thump. "Oh! What's this?"

"How do you like the wall that the others asked me to build?" the rotten builder asked as Ziggy, Trixie and Mayor Meanswell gathered around to inspect it. "You know, Sticky and, uh, Picky . . ."

14

Stingy and Pixel had asked for the wall?
Stephanie, Trixie and Ziggy couldn't believe it!

"They said something about not wanting to see you again," said the builder smugly. But before the friends could reply, he opened a door in the wall and disappeared inside.

"**T**his is outrageous," Stingy said scornfully. "They've cut me off from over half my town!"

Pixel had an idea. "There are still plenty of things to do on this side of the wall. What about soccer?"

"The goal is on their side," Stingy pointed out.

Trixie had the same idea – but all the soccer balls were on Stingy and Pixel's side!

The day was not going very well. "The worst part is, we can't have a birthday party for Sportacus," sighed Pixel.

Robbie looked on, amazed that his plan had worked!

Bessie Busybody had not forgotten Sportacus's special day and had brought along a birthday cake.

"Oh my!" she exclaimed to Stingy and Pixel. "Who put that giant wall there?"

"It was your friend the Mayor and all those on the other side," Stingy sulked . . . as sneaky Robbie stole the cake from under Bessie's nose!

"I was really looking forward to a piece of Miss Busybody's special birthday cake," the Mayor said sadly, as the cake landed right on his head with a splat!

Sportacus had not even begun to enjoy his day when his crystal beeped.

Straight away he flipped into the Skutla and zoomed down to LazyTown, where . . .

OOMF!

...e bumped into the wall!

..."What's this wall doing here?"
...portacus wondered. Then he
...oticed his friends, in the
...middle of a cake fight.

Sportacus frowned. His friends
shouldn't be fighting! He would
have to bring them together.

"I need sports candy to jump over this wall," Sportacus decided.
An apple shot out of the hatch of the airship and hurtled towards him.

But Robbie caught it first and sneakily swapped it for one filled
with sickly-sweet caramel. Poor Sportacus. When he took a
bite of the caramel apple and began to scale the wall,
he went into

sugar meltdown!

Ziggy was the first to see Sportacus, out cold on the top of the wall.

"Sportacus is in trouble!" he shouted.

Stephanie saw the candy apple lying on the ground and realised that Sportacus had been tricked into eating it. She would have to get him some sports candy fast!

But the apple tree was on the other side of the wall.

"We've got to work together," Stephanie told her friends.

So Pixel and Stephanie began to chisel through from either side of Robbie's rotten wall.

Robbie was not happy. His plan and his wall were falling apart! Everyone was co-operating!

Pah!

Stephanie broke through the wall to see Pixel, Stingy and Bessie for the first time that day.

"Boy, am I glad to see you!" Pixel declared, and everyone became friends again.

Stephanie quickly hatched a plan to save Sportacus. Pixel would kick his soccer ball into the apple tree to knock an apple into Stephanie's hands. Stephanie would climb the wall and feed Sportacus the sports candy.

The plan worked perfectly – almost!
At the top of the wall, Stephanie began to topple.

"Whoa!"

she cried, falling backwards.

Sportacus woke up just in time, and caught Stephanie's hand at the very last second!

Stephanie's friends breathed huge sighs of relief. "That was close, huh?" said Ziggy.

"Thank you, Sportacus!" said Stephanie as he lowered her to the ground.

"You're welcome. **But why is this big wall here?**" Sportacus asked.

Trixie peered through the hole in the wall at Stingy and Pixel. "They built it."

"We didn't build the giant wall," Stingy argued. "You asked for it to be built! He told me! The giant wall builder!"

Everyone looked over at where Stingy was pointing.

"Robbie Rotten!"
the friends all shouted at once.

"Uh, gotta go!" Robbie grimaced and sneaked away,
knowing he'd been foiled again!

Stephanie gave Stingy and Pixel a big hug.
"Guys, I'm really sorry we had a fight," she said.

"I'm sorry, too," said Stingy, and soon everybody was
apologising. In all the chaos of hugs and sorrys, Ziggy
found the birthday present that the friends had bought for
Sportacus – a super new skateboard! Sportacus loved it.

"How about we get rid of this wall?" Sportacus
suggested. It was his birthday, after all, and he
wanted all his friends in one place! 29

Stephanie skipped away and came back with another surprise for Sportacus.

"Happy Birthday!"

Stephanie sang as she gave him the cake she had made specially, full of fruit and vegetables – a sports candy cake! It was perfect, especially as Bessie's sugary cake was now in pieces all over LazyTown!

"A cake? For me?" Sportacus was thrilled.

Sportacus's friends cheered,

"Happy Birthday!"

and celebrated his special day the way that Sportacus wanted – together!

Stephanie Says, Stingy Says!

Why not play **Stephanie Says, Stingy Says?** It's not very different from **Simon Says**, but instead of everyone doing what one person says, everyone does what two people say!

Go find . . .

4+ friends to play with

Go play!

Choose one friend to be **Stephanie** and one friend to be **Stingy**. Make sure everyone takes turns at being the LazyTown friends! You can play to some cool upbeat music if you like – but make sure you **keep moving!**

Stephanie

should think of some cool dance moves to ask everyone to copy.
Try . . .
Clapping your hands!
Skipping on the spot!
High-kicking!
Jumping!

Stingy

should think of things to tell everyone to do. Try . . .
Taking two steps forwards!
Turning to your left!
Moving backwards!
Swapping places with the person on your right!

Stephanie calls out, "Stephanie says . . ." and chooses a dance move for everyone to follow. If Stephanie decides not to say, "Stephanie says . . ." and someone copies her dance move anyway, that person takes over as Stingy.

Next, Stingy calls out, "Stingy says . . ." and chooses something for everyone to do at the same time. If Stingy decides not to say, "Stingy says . . ." and someone does what he tells them to anyway, this person takes over as Stephanie.

This game can be played with lots of people following Stephanie's and Stingy's instructions at the same time, for example, jumping and moving backwards! It can get very confusing – which can be great fun!

"I feel like dancin'!"

Birthday
Hopscotch!

Birthday Hopscotch is like ordinary hopscotch but with a neat twist to keep you moving!

Go find...

A friend*
A soft object that won't bounce

*although you can also play **Birthday Hopscotch** by yourself!

Go play!

Draw a 12-box hopscotch grid with chalk on a pavement where it can be washed off, or on a big piece of paper that can be safely taped to the floor. See picture 1 on the opposite page.

Great! Now write the names of the months January to December
in the grid, from the bottom up, as in picture 2.

1

2

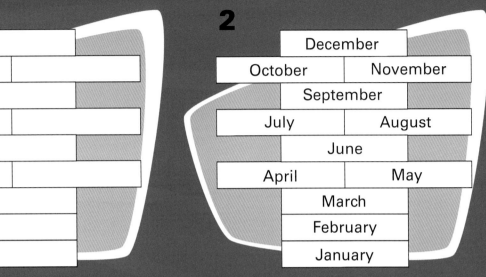

December	
October	November
September	
July	August
June	
April	May
March	
February	
January	

Finally, write the birthdates of all players in the box for the right month.
If your birthday is 12th June, write the number 12 in the 'June' box. If your friend's
birthday is 31st December, write the number 31 in the 'December' box.

Now you can play!

Throw a soft object onto the
grid and check out which box it
lands in. Hop all the way to that
box as fast as you can.

Here's the twist! If that box has
a number in it, hop that many
times in the box before you
continue your turn and hop
up and down the grid! So,
if you land on 'December'
and the number 31 is
written in the box, you
hop 31 times!

"That's what I call energy!"

Wall Ball

Wall Ball is a high-energy game you can play by yourself or with friends, and is great practice for other ball games!

Go find . . .

A ball
A plain wall with no windows
A friend*

*although you can also play **Wall Ball** by yourself!

Go play!

Begin by simply throwing the ball against the wall and catching it as it bounces back at you. Try this a few times until you feel more confident. If you are playing with a friend, stand next to each other. Take turns; throw the ball at the wall and let your friend catch it, then have them throw it at the wall for you to catch.

Playing with a few friends? Stand side by side and throw the ball at the wall for the friend next to you to catch. He should then throw the ball for the friend next to him to catch. When you reach the end of the row, throw the ball back along the row again.

Got it? Great!

Now try any – or all – of these different variations!

Clap!

Throw the ball and clap your hands before you catch it. Clap once first, then twice, then clap once more each time you throw the ball, until you reach 10. If you are playing with friends, see who reaches 10 claps first.

In Line!

A fast and frantic game for you to play with your friends! Line up facing the wall, one behind the other. The person at the front of the row throws the ball at the wall then runs to the back of the line, as the second person moves forward to catch the ball. This person throws the ball at the wall, runs to the back of the line so the third person catches the ball, and so on!

Spin to Win!

Throw the ball at the wall and try to spin on the spot before it bounces back at you!

"Let's move it, people!"

37

Memory Games

Why not play some memory games?
Can you remember . . .

Who . . .

1. . . . thought the sports field was the best place for a party?

2. . . . drew a chalk line to separate the friends?

3. . . . spotted Sportacus on top of the wall?

What . . .

1. . . . did Ziggy have on his finger to help him remember?

2. . . . was in the apple that Sportacus ate by accident?

3. . . . did Pixel use to knock an apple out of the tree?

?

Where . . .

. . . do these objects belong?

Can you find each one on a different page?

1

2

3

?

Spot the Difference

There are 5 differences between this picture and the picture on page 2. Can you spot them all in this picture?

40

Answers: Stingy is in the picture. Pixel is not in the picture. Stephanie has a blue stripe on her jumper. Trixie is missing the pattern on her top and the airship has appeared in the background.